NOTES FOR PARENTS

* Point to the words as you read them, then talk about the pictures together.

* What is happening in the pictures? Encourage your toddler to comment on the people and things he/she recognises.

* What will happen on *his/her* birthday?

Geraldine Taylor, Reading Consultant

Acknowledgment:
The publishers would like to thank Lynn Breeze for the cover illustration.

A catalogue record for this book is available
from the British Library

Published by Ladybird Books Ltd Loughborough Leicestershire UK
Ladybird Books Ltd is a subsidiary of the Penguin Group of companies
© LADYBIRD BOOKS LTD MCMXCII This edition MCMXCIV
LADYBIRD and the device of a Ladybird are trademarks of Ladybird Books Ltd

toddlers
It's my birthday

by HARRIET GRIFFEY
illustrated by COLIN KING

Time to get up.

What's special about today?
It's my birthday!

Wake up, Annie!
It's my birthday!

Hello, Dad.
It's my birthday!

It's my
birthday…
and today
I'm three.

Oh, a present for me?
Now, what can it be?

Are these all for me?

Hello, Grandpa.
It's my birthday!

We're going
to have
a party.

Hello, everybody!
It's my birthday.

Let's play some games.

I'm going to make a wish.

What a lovely birthday
I've had!